This book belongs to

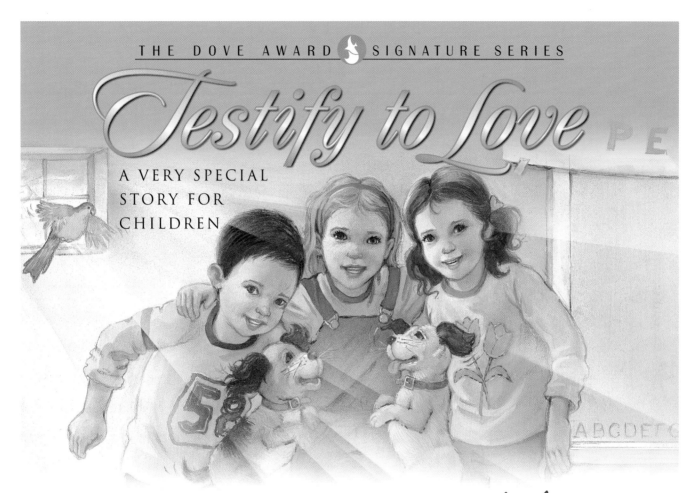

THE DOVE AWARD SIGNATURE SERIES

Testify to Love

A VERY SPECIAL
STORY FOR
CHILDREN

BASED ON THE DOVE AWARD™ SONG BY *Avalon*

STORY WRITTEN BY STEPHEN ELKINS · NARRATED BY JANNA LONG OF AVALON

ILLUSTRATED BY ELLIE COLTON

BROADMAN
& HOLMAN
PUBLISHERS

Nashville, Tennessee

With special thanks to Frank Breeden, Bonnie Pritchard, and the Gospel Music Association.

Song performed by the Wonder Kids Choir: Teri Deel, Emily Elkins, Laurie Evans, Tasha Goddard, Amy Lawrence, Lindsey McAdams, Lisa Harper, and Emily Walker. Solo performed by Emily Elkins.

Arranged and produced by Stephen Elkins.
CD recorded in a split-track format.

Testify To Love, words and music by Ralph Van Manen, Robert Riekerk, Henk Pool and Paul Field
© 1998 Universal-MCA Music Publishing, Inc. a division of Universal Studios, Inc. (ASCAP).
International copyright secured. All rights reserved.

Cover design and layout by Ed Maksimowicz.

Library of Congress Cataloging-in-Publication Data
Elkins, Stephen.
    Testify to love / by Stephen Elkins ; illustrations by Ellie Colton.
      p. cm. -- (Dove Award signature series)
    ISBN 0-8054-2416-4
    [1. Pets -- Fiction. 2. Creation -- Fiction. 3. Christian life -- Fiction.] I. Colton, Ellie, ill. II. Title. III. Series.

PZ7.E4282 Te 2002
[E] -- dc21

                                                                                              2001043324

ISBN 0-8054-2416-4

1 2 3 4 5   06 05 04 03 02

*This book is lovingly dedicated to
Cora Monday Burgess, my grandmother,
whose life has been a testimony
of God's faithfulness and unfailing love.*

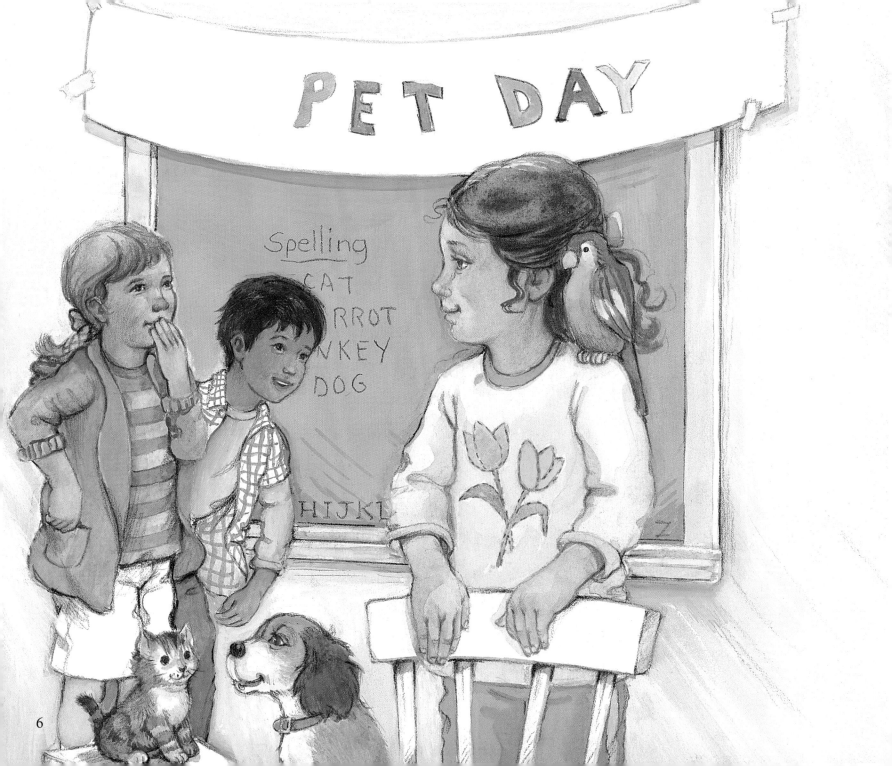

6

All the colors of the rainbow.

There were reds, blues, greens, even a splash of yellow on Tutu. Tutu was Bonnie's pet parrot. He was a very colorful and beautiful bird. Yes, it was Pet Day and all the kids agreed that it was their favorite school day of all.

All the voices of the wind.

And the chatter of the kids filled the school like a storm. Their teacher, Mrs. Garrett, directed the parade of pets. For many, this was the first time they'd ever seen some of these exciting and unusual animals.

PET DAY

Spelling
CAT
PARROT
MoNKEY
DoG

BCDEFGHIJKLM

9

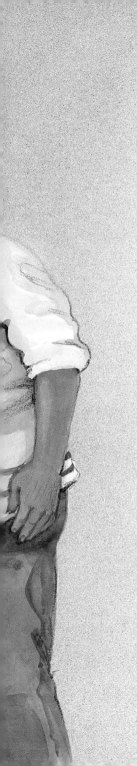

*Every dream
that reaches out,
that reaches out to find
where love begins.*

TESTIFY TO LOVE

"I just love seeing all the animals," Bonnie exclaimed. "Especially the little lamb, he's so cuddly. We were just studying about David, the shepherd boy, this past Sunday. Why he must have had a hundred lambs to watch over."

Every word
of every story.

"And in the story David protected his sheep against a big bear," Rachel added. "He was very brave. Our Sunday school teacher said David protected his sheep because he loved them, just like God protects and loves us."

*Every star
in every sky.*

"Stars are what Owlfred sees every night," said Marty, describing his pet owl. "Did you know that while we're sleeping, Owlfred is wide awake, ready to eat and play? God gave him special eyes to see in the dark," he said.

Marty explained to the group that Owlfred was injured as a baby, so Marty's parents taught him all about owls so he could take care of him.

*Every corner
of creation lives
to testify.*

"All these pets are so wonderful!" exclaimed Bonnie. "From Tutu to Owlfred, God's creation is so amazing."

"And don't forget he created us, too," Rachel reminded Bonnie. "As Pastor Morgan always says, 'We're God's prized creation and a testimony to His love.'"

"What is that chorus we sing that says all creation testifies to God's love?" asked Bonnie.

17

For as long as I shall live, I will testify to love. I'll be a witness in the silences when words are not enough.

Rachel and Bonnie sang. "To think God created everything in just six days," Bonnie said.

Just then the door to the classroom opened. In burst Jesse carrying the funniest looking pet they'd ever seen. Then Jesse announced, "Ladies and gentlemen, would you welcome Darwin, the musical monkey, a million years in the making."

Darwin sat upon a music box turning a little crank that made music.

19

With every breath I take, I will give thanks to God above. For as long as I shall live, I will testify to love.

"And Darwin is surely a testimony to God's sense of humor," said Bonnie, looking at the funny little monkey. "Where did you get him, Jesse?"

"Oh, my uncle gave him to me," Jesse explained. But…

22

TESTIFY TO LOVE

"Everything, including Mr. Darwin here, evolved over millions of years," Jesse said. Then he held Darwin out and the girls got a closer look. "Just look at his face," he continued. "Darwin is actually one of our ancestors. He evolved just like we did. Isn't that amazing?"

From the river to the sea.

"Amazing," Rachel spoke up. "I know what evolve means and it's amazing that you could believe such a thing. Instead of God creating everything with purpose, evolve means that everything came to be all by itself, without God's help. All these animals didn't evolve, Jesse. God created each and every one of them, with purpose and design."

PET DAY

Spelling
CAT
PARROT
MONKEY
DOG

GDEFGHIJI

*Every hand
that reaches out,
every hand that reaches
out to offer peace.*

TESTIFY TO LOVE

As Rachel reached out to pet Darwin, he suddenly grabbed her lunch bag which contained the banana she had brought for lunch. As Rachel stood frozen Darwin snatched the banana, jumped onto Bonnie's head, then propelled himself to the top of the classroom door.

Every simple act of mercy, every step to kingdom come.

"I can't believe we've been outwitted by a monkey," Bonnie said. But there sat Darwin on top of the door, enjoying the banana. "Well, we have to remember God created him, too," Rachel said.

"Not created," said Jesse. "Evolved. Scientists say that Darwin evolved."

"Not all scientists," countered Rachel. "There are many scientists who believe that God created all things, and it's easy to understand why. Jesse do you believe Darwin's music box evolved, too? I mean, did it come together all by itself?"

PET DAY

Spelling
CAT
PARROT
MONKEY
DOG

ABCDEFGHIJK XYZ

30

All the hope in every heart will speak what love has done.

"That's silly," said Jesse. "It was made by a very smart person. Look at how all these parts fit together so perfectly. Oh, I think I'm beginning to see what you mean. How could an entire universe just evolve when a music box couldn't?"

Just then Tutu the parrot, who'd been quiet, flew off his perch and landed on the handle of the music box. As if on cue, Darwin started turning the handle. The kids laughed as the parrot went up and down.

Bonnie, Rachel, and Jesse agreed this had been the best Pet Day ever, and Jesse began to see that all creation does testify to God's love.

Don't miss the other titles in the Dove Award™ Signature Series for Children

The Great Adventure
*Based on the Dove Award™ Song
by Steven Curtis Chapman*

0-8054-2399-0

Thank You
*Based on the Dove Award™ Song
by Ray Boltz*

0-8054-2400-8

God is In Control
*Based on the Dove Award™ Song
by Twila Paris*

0-8054-2402-4

Available at Christian Bookstores everywhere.